Goodnight, Moon Baby

By Andrew Davenport

Copyright © 2019 Moon and Me

Scholastic Children's Books,
Euston House, 24 Eversholt Street,
London NW1 1DB, UK

A division of Scholastic Ltd
London ~ New York ~ Toronto ~ Sydney ~ Auckland
Mexico City ~ New Delhi ~ Hong Kong

Published in the UK by Scholastic Ltd, 2019

ISBN 978 1407 18854 6

Printed and bound in Italy

2 4 6 8 10 9 7 5 3 1

The right of Andrew Davenport to be identified as the author of this work respectively has been asserted
by him in accordance with the Copyright, Designs and Patents Act, 1988.

www.scholastic.co.uk

Moon Baby lives
on the Moon.

Hello, Moon Baby!

When Moon Baby gets a letter from his friend, Pepi Nana, he puts on his gloves, pulls up his hood, and flies down to visit.

Look up to the sky – you might see him go by!

"Tiddle toddle!"

Hello Pepi Nana! Pepi Nana and
Moon Baby are best friends.

Moon Baby plays a tune on his
magical kalimba to wake up all
the toy friends.

Wake up, Mr Onion. **"Onions!"**

Wake up, Dibillo. **"Yawn!"**

Wake up, Little Nana. **"Poop-poop!"**

Wake up, Lambkin. **"Baa! Baa!"**

Wake up, Colly Wobble. **"Tinkle-tinkle!"**

Wake up, Lily Plant. **"Oh, my dears!"**

The Toy House is awake!

The friends are very happy to see Moon Baby.
They love to share a new story together.

Moon Baby plays a
magical tune on his
kalimba to take us
to Storyland.

Hold hands!

Storyland. Where many stories wait for Moon Baby, Pepi Nana and their Toy House friends.

Sometimes they
visit a big castle.

Sometimes they race.

Sometimes they go exploring together.

And sometimes they cross Mr Onion's bridge.

And do you know what Moon Baby, Pepi Nana
and their friends do after every story?
They play music together!

Today they are singing:

So many stories
Wait for us each day –
Every day
A way to say
'I love you!'

Then Moon Baby plays his magical kalimba once again.
The Toy House! Time to go home.

"Oh, my dears!" says Lily Plant. "Just in time for tea!"
"We can have tea every day when Moon Baby
comes to visit," says Little Nana.
And everybody thinks she is right about that.

After tea everybody yawns a big yawn.
"Hush, hush," says the Moon. **"It's time to go to sleep**."
Moon Baby plays his magical music.

Goodnight,
Mr Onion.

Goodnight,
Dibillo.

Goodnight,
Colly Wobble.

Goodnight, Lily
Plant.

Goodnight,
Little Nana.

Goodnight,
Lambkin.

Moon Baby and Pepi Nana say goodbye, until tomorrow.

Moon Baby flies back to the Moon.

Goodnight, Pepi Nana!

Goodnight, Moon Baby!